Scan this QR Code on
your smartphone for
a free audio reading
of this book!

 let colour speak    @letcolourspeak

www.letcolourspeak.com

Dedicated to
Carmen Theresa Jarrett
& all the wise souls
I know

MIAUW!
Every DAWG ave im Day, Every PUSS ave HIM 4 'CLOCK!
WOOf
MIAUW!

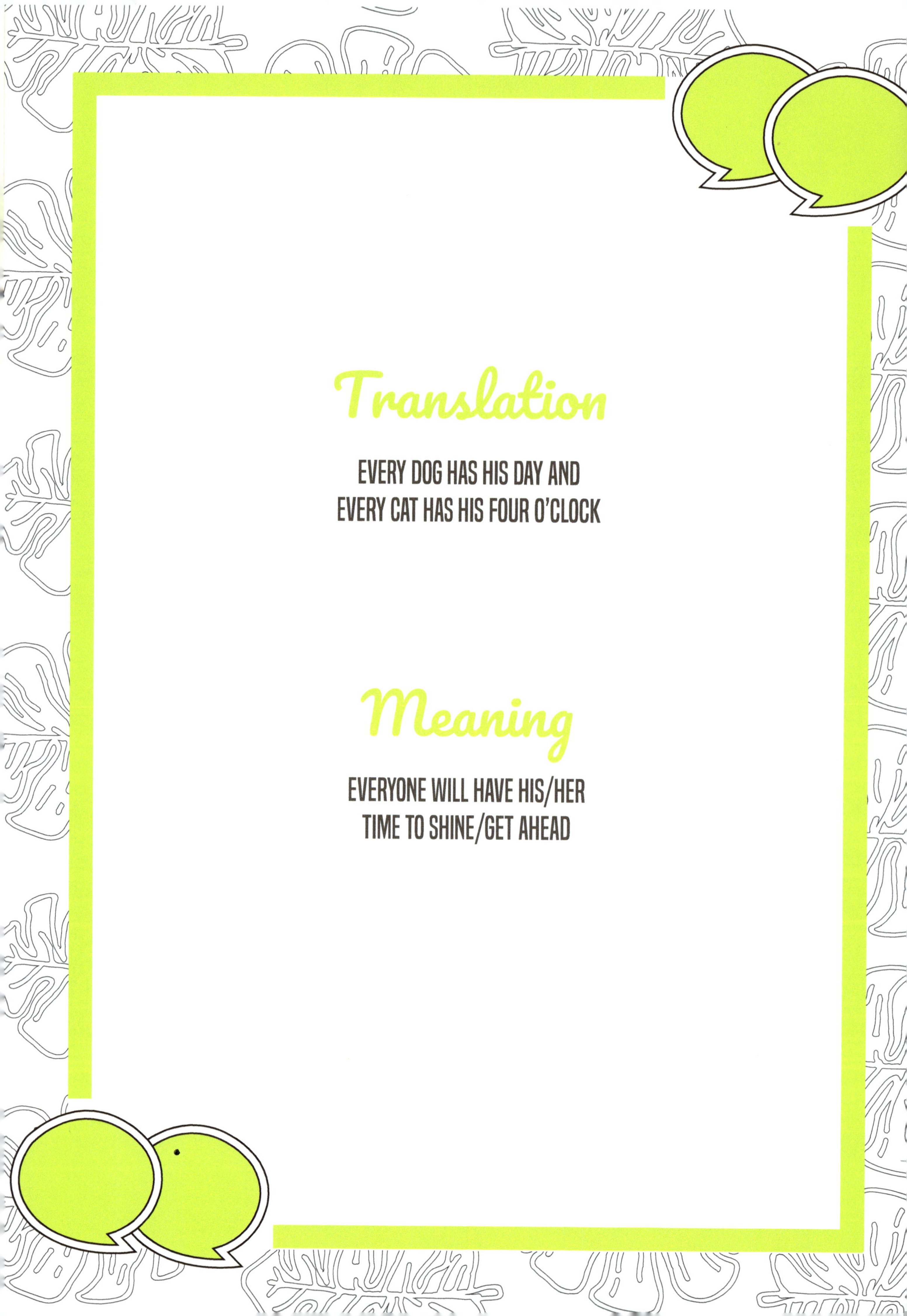

Translation

EVERY DOG HAS HIS DAY AND
EVERY CAT HAS HIS FOUR O'CLOCK

Meaning

EVERYONE WILL HAVE HIS/HER
TIME TO SHINE/GET AHEAD

WANTI
cyah get eh, getti
getti nuh want eh

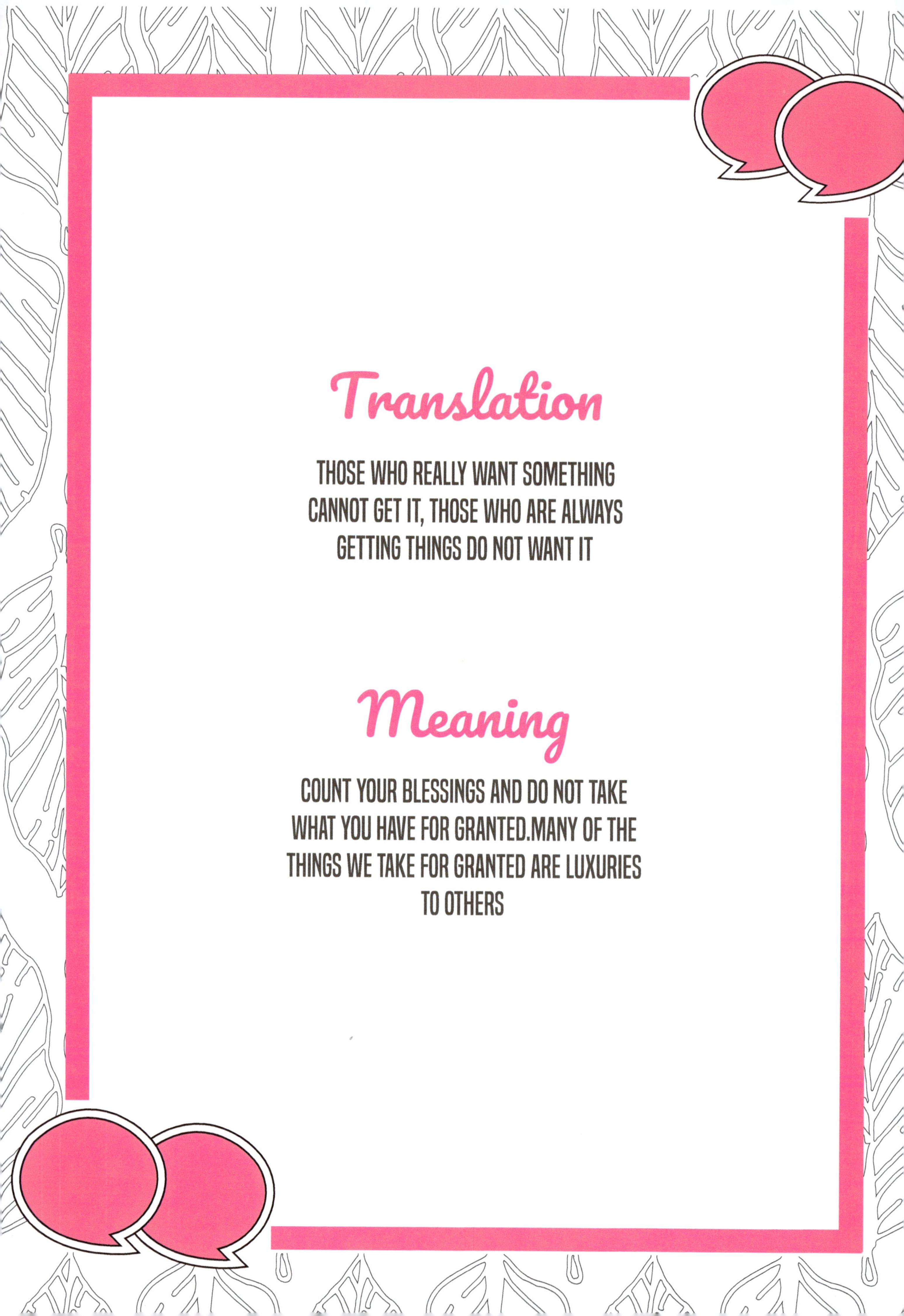

Translation

THOSE WHO REALLY WANT SOMETHING
CANNOT GET IT, THOSE WHO ARE ALWAYS
GETTING THINGS DO NOT WANT IT

Meaning

COUNT YOUR BLESSINGS AND DO NOT TAKE
WHAT YOU HAVE FOR GRANTED.MANY OF THE
THINGS WE TAKE FOR GRANTED ARE LUXURIES
TO OTHERS

MI CUM yah
FI DRINK
Milk
MI NUH
CUM yah FI
COUNT COW

Translation

I CAME HERE TO DRINK MILK,
I DIDN'T COME TO COUNT COWS

Meaning

WE SHOULD CONDUCT BUSINESS IN A
STRAIGHTFORWARD MANNER.
IT ALSO MEANS THAT YOU SHOULD DELIVER
WHAT YOU PROMISE
AND NOT WASTE TIME TALKING ABOUT IT.

Nuh WAIT
Till DRUM
BEAT
BEFORE
YUH
GRIN' YUH
AXE

Translation

DO NOT WAIT UNTIL THE DRUM BEATS
BEFORE YOU GRIND YOUR AXE

Meaning

BE PREPARED FOR ALL EVENTUALITIES;
DO NOT WAIT UNTIL IT IS TOO LATE

Wah Sweet Nanny Goat, Ah Guh Run Him Belly

Translation

WHAT TASTES GOOD TO A GOAT
WILL LATER UPSET HIS STOMACH

Meaning

THE THINGS THAT SEEM FINE TO
YOU NOW CAN HURT YOU LATER.

If Yuh
Wan
Good
Yuh Fi
Nose
Haffi Run

Translation

IF YOU WANT GOOD, YOUR NOSE
WILL HAVE TO RUN

Meaning

IN ORDER TO GET GOOD THINGS OUT OF LIFE,
YOU MUST BE PREPARED TO DEAL WITH
UNCOMFORTABLE/UNPLEASANT SITUATIONS
ALONG THE WAY

Poun' ah fret
cyaan pay ownce ah dett
£

Translation

ONE POUND OF FRETTING CANNOT
REPAY ONE OUNCE OF DEBTS

Meaning

PROBLEMS ARE NOT SOLVED BY WORRYING.

EXIT
EF YUH CYAAN TAN BUN CUT AN RUN

Translation

IF YOU CAN'T TAKE A BURN,
CUT AND RUN

Meaning

GET OUT OF ANY SITUATION IN WHICH YOU
FEEL THREATENED OR PRESSURED INTO
DOING ANYTHING AGAINST YOUR WILL

The Older The Moon, The Brighter It Shine

Translation

THE OLDER THE MOON, THE BRIGHTER
IT SHINES

Meaning

PEOPLE (AND THINGS) GET
BETTER WITH AGE

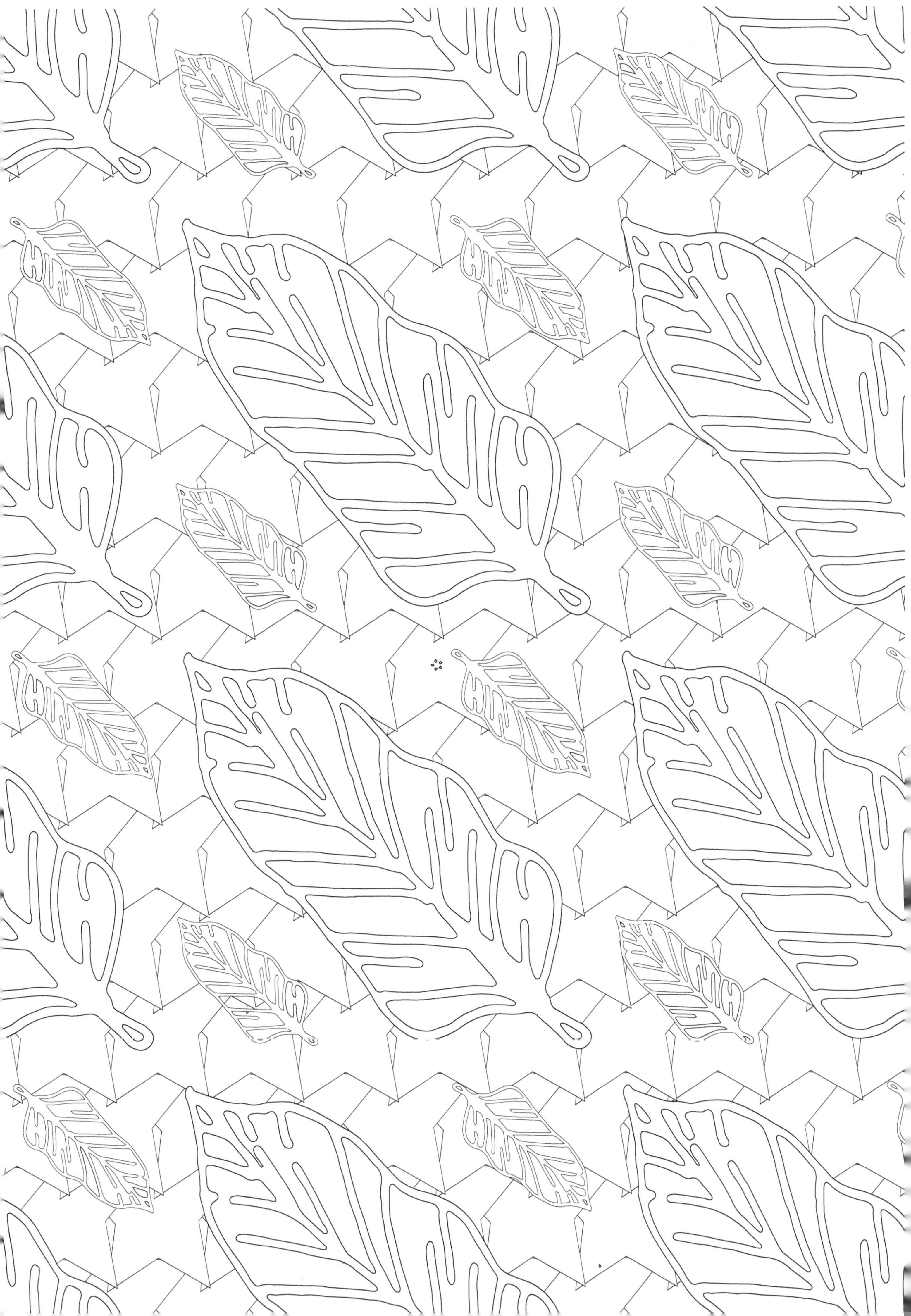

Youngbud nuh know storm

Translation

YOUNG BIRDS KNOW NOTHING
ABOUT STORMS

Meaning

WITH AGE COMES WISDOM
AND EXPERIENCE

BAD
FAMBILY
IS BETTO
Dan
EMPTY
PIGSTY

Translation

A BAD FAMILY IS BETTER
THAN AN EMPTY PIGSTY

Meaning

FAMILY IS IMPORTANT. NO MATTER HOW
BAD YOU THINK THEY ARE, YOU SHOULD
TREASURE THEM

GOOD
FREN
BETTA
DAN
POCKET MONEY

Translation

A GOOD FRIEND IS BETTER
THAN MONEY IN THE POCKET

Meaning

A GOOD FRIEND, ESPECIALLY IN TIMES
OF TROUBLE, IS ALWAYS PROVEN TO BE
OF MUCH MORE WORTH

CHICKEN
MERRY
MERRY
HAWK
DEH
NEAR
Cluck
Cluck
Cluck

Translation

CHICKEN IS MERRY, A HAWK
IS NEARBY

Meaning

EVERY SILVER LINING HAS ITS DARK
CLOUDS. EVEN IN THE HAPPIEST TIME
ONE MUST BE WATCHFUL

Learn
BEFORE
to
CREEP
YUH
walk

Translation

LEARN TO CRAWL BEFORE YOU WALK

Meaning

LEARN THE BASICS BEFORE YOU TRY TO
DO THINGS THAT ARE MORE COMPLEXED.
TAKE THINGS ONE STEP AT A TIME

Cockroach
nuh business
inna fowl fight

Translation

COCKROACHES SHOULD NOT
CONCERN THEMSELVES WITH FIGHTS
BETWEEN CHICKENS/FOWLS

Meaning

STAY OUT OF SITUATIONS THAT
HAVE NOTHING TO DO WITH YOU!

Mi Old
But Mi
Nuh
Cold

Translation

I AM OLD BUT I AM NOT COLD

Meaning

THIS WARNS US NOT TO UNDERESTIMATE
THE VALUE OF THE ELDERLY

EVERY MIKKLE
MEKA MUKKLE

Translation

EVERY LITTLE MAKES SOMETHING

Meaning

EVERY PENNY SAVED IS A
PENNY EARNED

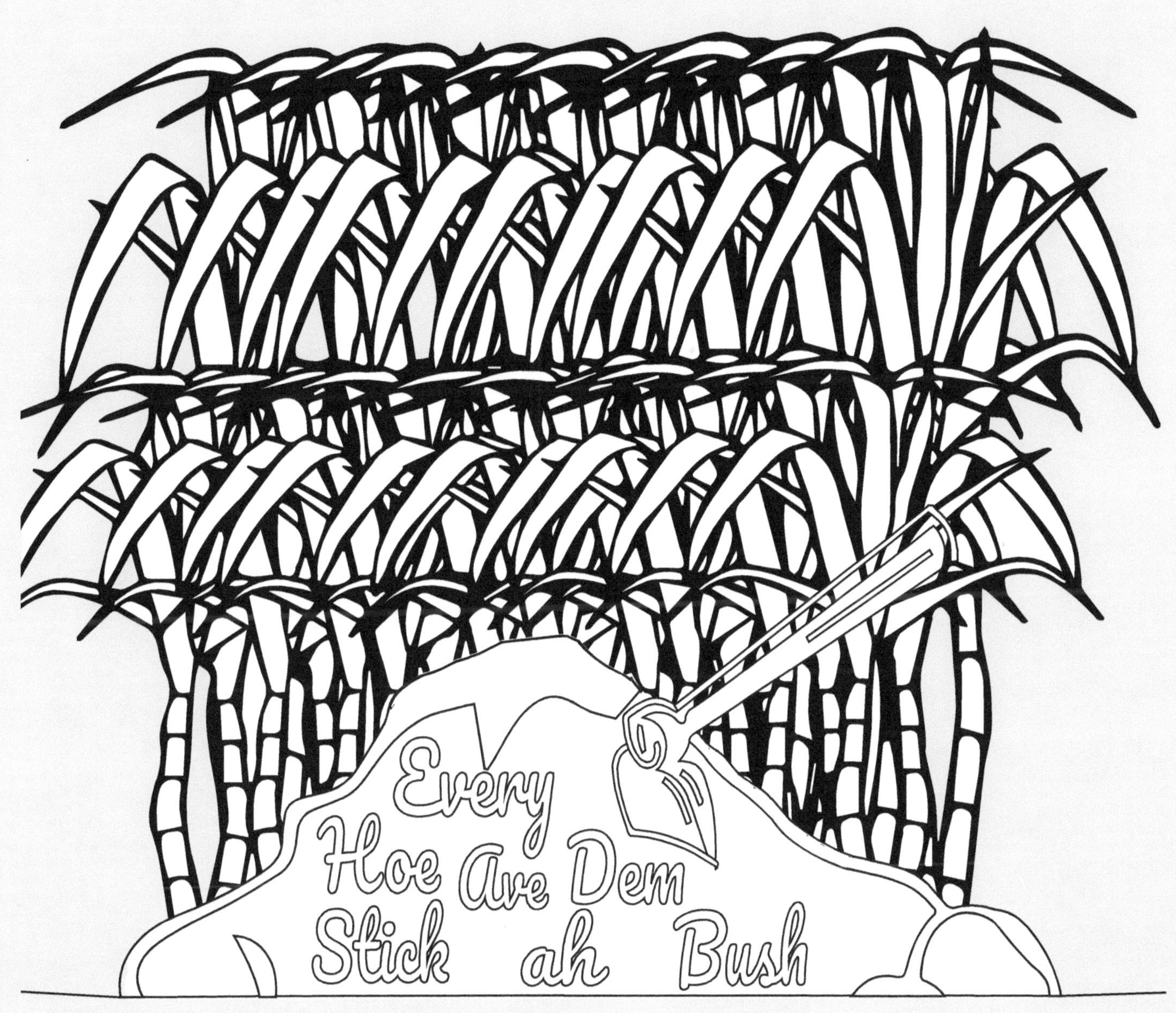

Every
Hoe Ave Dem
Stick ah Bush

Translation

EVERY HOE HAS THEIR
THICKET OF BUSHES

Meaning

THERE IS SOMEONE FOR
EVERYONE

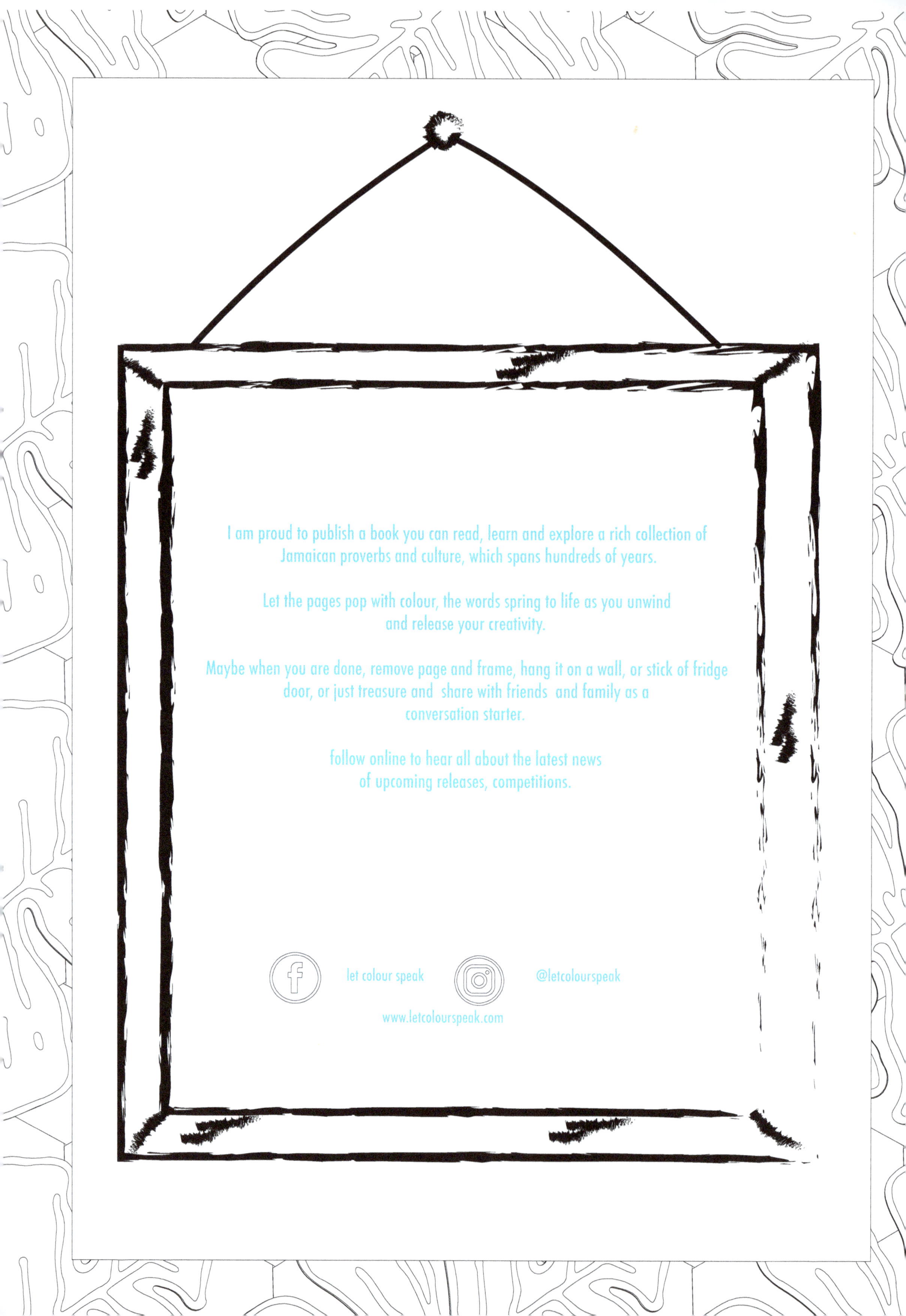

I am proud to publish a book you can read, learn and explore a rich collection of
Jamaican proverbs and culture, which spans hundreds of years.

Let the pages pop with colour, the words spring to life as you unwind
and release your creativity.

Maybe when you are done, remove page and frame, hang it on a wall, or stick of fridge
door, or just treasure and share with friends and family as a
conversation starter.

follow online to hear all about the latest news
of upcoming releases, competitions.

let colour speak   @letcolourspeak
www.letcolourspeak.com